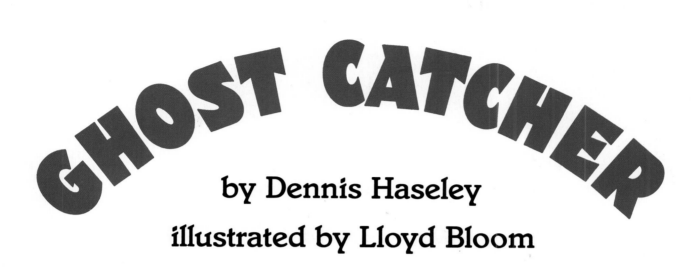

GHOST CATCHER

by Dennis Haseley

illustrated by Lloyd Bloom

For Rob Klotz
D.H.

To my mother and father
L.B.

Ghost Catcher
Text copyright © 1991 by Dennis Haseley
Illustrations copyright © 1991 by Lloyd Bloom
Printed in the U.S.A. All rights reserved.
Typography by Al Cetta
1 2 3 4 5 6 7 8 9 10
First Edition

Library of Congress Cataloging-in-Publication Data
Haseley, Dennis.
  Ghost catcher / by Dennis Haseley ; illustrated by Lloyd Bloom.
    p.   cm.
  "A Laura Geringer book."
  Summary: An allegory of emotional growth and human kinship in
which Ghost Catcher solves people's problems and they in turn help
him.
  ISBN 0-06-022244-1.—ISBN 0-06-022247-6 (lib. bdg.)
  [1. Friendship—Fiction.   2. Shadows—Fiction.   3. Allegories.]
I. Bloom, Lloyd, ill.   II. Title.
PZ7.H2688Gh   1991   91-4426
[E]—dc20   CIP
                                                       AC

■ A Laura Geringer Book

An Imprint of HarperCollins*Publishers*

Ghost Catcher could get close to ghosts without turning into one. He looked like anyone, except he didn't have a shadow. Not in the sun, not by a candle, not even standing by a fire. No shadow. He said that was because he was never scared and never mad and never sad.

Ghost Catcher was sitting out, listening to his friend the man who played the trumpet. A boy walked up, said, "I've got to talk to you."

"Looks like business," said the man with the trumpet, and walked away.

The boy looked this way and that, said, "My dog's gone."

Ghost Catcher asked, "You love your dog?"

The boy said, "Yeah, but I treated him bad."

Ghost Catcher asked how.

The boy said, "He made me so mad I hit him with a stick. So I guess he got sad and died."

Ghost Catcher asked, "What do you love most in this world, next to your dog?"

The boy said, "Sugarcane candy."

Ghost Catcher said, "Okay, bring me all you have, and the stick you hit your dog with."

The boy went away, brought back the stick and a big sack of sugarcane candy.

"That all?" asked Ghost Catcher.

The boy took out three more pieces.

Ghost Catcher walked away, out over the hills, past the cactus standing with spikes, walked far away from where the village was. He started feeling tired, and he put a piece of sugarcane candy in his mouth. He kept walking.

Ghost Catcher started to hear panting, like it was coming from the air. He sat down. Now he saw, sweeping over the hills like the shadow of a cloud, the shadow of a dog. Ghost Catcher watched that shadow run around and around him, listened to that panting.

Ghost Catcher reached into the sack, took out a piece of candy, ate it. "I sure do love that sugarcane candy," said Ghost Catcher. That dog shadow was running around and around.

"Yeah, I sure do love that sugarcane candy," said Ghost Catcher, and he ate another piece.

Then he picked up the stick and WHAP, he hit the sack a good one. "Yeah, I love that sugarcane candy," he said. WHAP, he hit the sack with the stick again. The ghost dog was running around faster now, panting harder. Ghost Catcher looked in the sack. "Oh no," said Ghost Catcher. "My sugarcane candy's all crumbled up and sad looking."

Now that shadow dog stopped running, his shadow head cocked. Ghost Catcher said, "Boy told me he lost his best old dog. Said if he had that dog back he'd never hit it with a stick again. Too bad that dog'll never know."

That shadow came closer. Out of the corner of his eye, Ghost Catcher could see a spot of sun in its two black eyes, he could see parts of that black shadow becoming black hair. Ghost Catcher knew he'd stopped that dog from going wherever it was going.

Ghost Catcher stood up, threw away the stick. He picked up that sack of sugarcane candy, started walking back to the village, back through the hills, past the cactus standing with spikes.

Ghost Catcher heard that dog panting behind him. He knew that for every step that dog looked less like a shadow, was more full of meat, bones, hair. He knew that the love of the boy was going back into that poor dog's heart. But he didn't turn around and look. He just went home.

Ghost Catcher sat out on his porch all that morning. He saw the boy run by, saw that dog following.

"Howdy," said the boy, stopping.

"Hello," said Ghost Catcher.

"Thanks," said the boy.

"Okay," said Ghost Catcher. "You know that sugarcane candy sure is good," he said. The boy laughed and ran off. That dog looked up at Ghost Catcher with his bright eyes, then he ran off, after his boy. "It's good in whole pieces," said Ghost Catcher, and he popped some into his mouth.

Ghost Catcher walked through the village. He wanted to be with his friends. He visited the pretty woman who was weaving a rug of many colors. They sat in her garden, drinking tea.

"Tell me," said the woman, "where was the ghost dog going?"

"I caught him before he got there," said Ghost Catcher. "So it's nothing I need to worry."

"It's something for *me* to worry," said the woman, "me with a shadow and you without."

Ghost Catcher laughed and got up. He started walking back to his house.

He passed two boys telling jokes to each other. "Hey," they said, "come play with us like you do." But Ghost Catcher's thoughts were far away. Maybe he would find out where the ghost dog had been going. He went to his porch and smoked his pipe. And on the ground beneath him, there was no shadow.

An old woman walked up to Ghost Catcher. "My old man's gone," she said.

Ghost Catcher asked, "You love your old man?"

The old woman said, "Yeah, but I treat him mean."

Ghost Catcher asked how.

The old woman said, "I'm always sweeping and tidying, tidying and sweeping, don't let him get any peace. Always make him move the one chair he's sitting in so I can sweep, always make him clean up the clean walls. Oh, I don't get any peace either," she said.

Ghost Catcher said, "Okay, next to your old man, what do you love most in the world?"

The old woman said, "Coffee bean."

Ghost Catcher said, "Bring me all you have. And bring me a pail of mud you cleaned from your house."

The old woman went away and came back with these things.

Ghost Catcher walked away, out over the hills, past the cactus standing with spikes, walked far away from the village. He started feeling tired, he put a coffee bean in his mouth. He kept walking. He walked until he came to that old man, in the middle of the hot heat, sitting by a fire, resting. The old man looked like a shadow, in the middle of the day.

"Hello," said Ghost Catcher.

"Oh my," said the old man.

"So where are you going?" asked Ghost Catcher.

The man pointed ahead. "I'm going there," said he.

Ghost Catcher looked and looked. He couldn't see a thing. Then the old man like a shadow shivered and said, "Feeling so thin. So cold." The old man started to cry and looked ahead, to where he was going, to where Ghost Catcher couldn't see.

That's when Ghost Catcher said, "Your woman sent me with this," and he reached in the bucket, smeared mud all over him. Made him solid.

Ghost Catcher carried that old man back through the hills, past the cactus standing with spikes.

He brought the old man back to his woman.

She said, "Oh! But he's all covered with mud."

Ghost Catcher said, "That's how he is now."

The old woman ran up to kiss her old man, and she got mud all over her dress.

Ghost Catcher walked through the village. He wanted to be with his friends again. He went to the girl who danced with bells on her arms and legs. He watched her dance, with her shadow dancing behind her. "It was good what you did for the old man," she whispered. "But tell me, where was the old man going?"

"I caught him before he got there," said Ghost Catcher, "so it's nothing I need to worry."

"It's something for *me* to worry," said the girl, "me with a shadow and you without."

This time Ghost Catcher did not laugh. Slowly, he walked back to his house, wondering where the old man had been going. He went to his porch, smoked his pipe. There was darkness in his head, and on the ground beneath him, there was no shadow.

The next day, he went to visit the woman weaving her rug of many colors. Ghost Catcher said, "I'm going to the place where ghosts go."

She said, "Don't do that, you won't come back. For who will catch you?"

"I don't need anyone to catch me," he said, "you with a shadow and me without. I'll just go there and have a look, and be home in time for tea."

"Well, then take this," she said, and she picked up the flowers she used to dye her wool.

But he shook his head. "I'm Ghost Catcher," he reminded her, and walked off.

He went to the girl who danced. Ghost Catcher said, "I'm going to the place where ghosts go."

She said, "Don't do that, you won't come back. For who will catch you?"

"I don't need anyone to catch me," he said with a smile.

"Well, then take this," she said, and she took the bells from her arms and legs.

But he said, "I'm Ghost Catcher," and walked off.

He went to the man who played the trumpet. "I'm going to the place where ghosts go," he said.

The man was going to say, "Don't do that, you won't come back," but he saw that Ghost Catcher had made up his mind. So he said, "Well, if you must go, then take this," and he handed him his trumpet.

But Ghost Catcher just said, "No thank you," and walked off.

And as he was walking to his house, he passed the boys playing in the street.

"We hear you're going away," they said.

Ghost Catcher nodded.

"We'll give you a joke to take," they said.

Ghost Catcher shook his head. "I'll bring a joke back for you," he said, and walked off.

Ghost Catcher sat in his house as the sun went down. "I want to go, I want to go, I want to go to the place where ghosts go," he whispered into the darkness. Then he made a cup of tea and waited. And for the first time he could remember, he felt scared.

One long night went by, and when morning came it was gray, and no birds were singing. Ghost Catcher heard a knock on his door and he jumped. He opened it, and there was a man wearing gray clothes, with a white cloth over his face.

"Hello," said the man, and his voice sounded like it was coming out of a long reed.

Ghost Catcher looked at the man, up and down. "You look like someone I know," he said, "but you're all covered up."

The man told Ghost Catcher to leave his house and walk out of the village. So Ghost Catcher did. He and the man just kept on walking. And everything seemed gray, and no birds were singing.

They walked out over the hills, past the cactus standing with spikes. "You do not need to turn around," said the man. "I will tell you where to walk."

Ghost Catcher thought, I will do what he says. They walked past a tree with green leaves on the near side and branches bleached and white as bones on the far side.

They walked farther into the desert. Up ahead, hanging from a cactus, was a suit of clothes, all in gray with a white cloth.

"Put on these clothes," said the man, "because of the sun. And put this cloth over your face, because of the wind."

And Ghost Catcher did.

When the sun was high in the sky, Ghost Catcher saw a dark shape ahead of him. He saw it grow darker and darker until he saw that he was entering a village made of shadows.

The man touched Ghost Catcher on the shoulder. "Ghost Catcher," he said. "Come, and look how it is here."

So the two, in their gray clothes, with white cloths over their faces, walked through the streets of the shadow village. Ghost Catcher saw the shadow of the old man, and the boy with his dog. "But I caught them before they became ghosts," he said to the man.

"You stopped them from joining their shadows," said the man. "But their shadows are still here, waiting."

"Hey, hello," Ghost Catcher said. They did not answer but stared straight ahead. And for the first time he could remember, Ghost Catcher felt mad.

He walked farther through the shadow of his village, toward the shadow of the pretty woman weaving a rug that was all gray. He climbed her steps, sat on her porch, and said, "Let's have some tea." But she just sat before her gray rug and did not pay him any mind.

I'm glad I do not have to stay here, Ghost Catcher thought angrily.

He walked toward the shadow of his own house, and there he saw the two boys in the street, not playing, just floating like two boys made of fog. He started to run toward them, but the man put his hand on his shoulder.

"They cannot hear or see you," he said. "To them, you are a ghost."

Suddenly, Ghost Catcher did not feel angry anymore. He felt sad. He turned to the man. "I want to go back now," he said. "I have seen enough of this village."

"This is your home now, Ghost Catcher," said the man, in his thin voice. "For who will catch you?"

Ghost Catcher hung his head. Now he knew where ghosts lived. And he knew how they lived. They lived always alone.

He sat down in the dirt, and as he did, the clothes of the man collapsed in a heap. Ghost Catcher saw his own shadow standing before him.

"Now you see that you have a shadow too," said his shadow. "You will get to know me very well."

Ghost Catcher knew he was becoming a shadow, and there was no one who could save him. He could see the shadows around him growing larger and darker. He thought of the village he had left; it had never seemed more beautiful. He thought of the friends he had turned away; he had never loved them more.

Tears came to his eyes and ran down his cheeks. He cried, but he knew there was no one who could hear him.

Then, from behind him, a trumpet began to blow soft, deep notes.

And in the air around him, flowers were blowing and scattering.

And next to him, almost in his ear, a boy's voice said, "What happens when a ghost sits in the sun too long?"

And another boy's voice answered, "You get *roast ghost.*"

Ghost Catcher looked around him. Trumpet notes were sweeping through the village of shadow. Wild ginger and daffodils, irises, and columbines the color of blood filled the air.

The boys' laughing voices tore through that gray village like a gale. And the shadows and the dark buildings fell before them like cards.

Now Ghost Catcher saw his own shadow sweeping toward him. But he heard the bells of the girl who danced. So he jumped to his feet. He saw his shadow stop, and tremble.

Ghost Catcher danced, waving his arms, kicking his legs, and that shadow began to cry, such a lonely sound, from so far away. Still Ghost Catcher danced, his gray clothes falling in tatters around him. His shadow grew flatter and flatter and fell to the earth.

And still Ghost Catcher danced.

He danced until he felt his friends around him, dancing with him, and he looked around now and saw he was back in his own village, and the shadow village was just shadows on the ground.

"You brought me back!" he shouted to his friends.

"You gave us some fright," said the woman with the rug of many colors, "wearing those funny clothes."

"You looked like you didn't know any of us," said the girl who danced. "You just kept looking at the shadows like you were in some kind of spell."

"So when you started to cry," said the man with the trumpet, "I blew a few notes at you."

"And I showed you my flowers."

"And we told you a good joke."

"And I danced for you."

Ghost Catcher looked them in the eye, one by one. "I was in the place where ghosts go," he said.

"Oh no," said the man with the trumpet. "That place is far away."

"Far away," said the women.

"Far away," said the boys.

"We're just glad you're all right now," said his friends.

After a little while, they said good-bye. Ghost Catcher watched them go their ways, one by one. He saw the pretty woman walk onto her porch, wave at him, and then sit down at her rug of many colors. He heard the birds singing.

He walked slowly back to his house, and then he saw that on the ground beside him was his shadow. Ghost Catcher nodded.

He climbed his steps and stood on his porch. He looked this way and that, saw his friends talking and joking.

"Come, and look at how it is here," he said to his shadow. "This is your home now."

Then he raised his arms wide until his arms circled his whole village.

Pretty soon a man walked up to him.

"You Ghost Catcher?" he asked.

Ghost Catcher nodded. "You with a shadow and me with a shadow," he said.

"My woman's gone," said the man.

Ghost Catcher looked at the man. "You love your woman?" he asked.

"Yeah, but I treat her bad," said the man.

Ghost Catcher smiled. "You and I, we better go get her," he said.

And they did.